Monsters Come in Many Colors!

by Jocelyn Stevenson

pictures by
Sammis McLean

A SESAME STREET BOOK/GOLDEN PRESS BOOK
Published by Western Publishing Company, Inc.
in conjunction with Children's Television Workshop

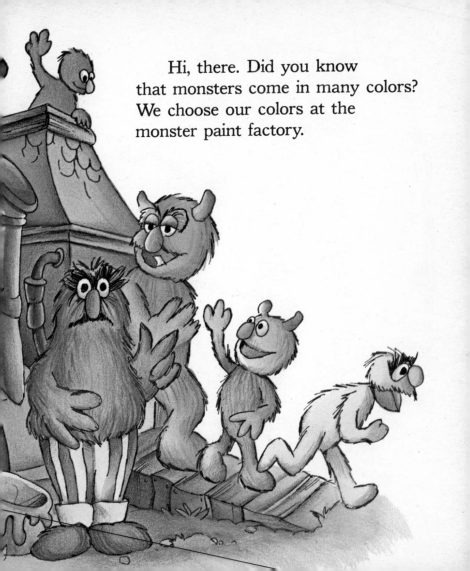

Hi, there. Did you know
that monsters come in many colors?
We choose our colors at the
monster paint factory.

Some monsters choose red.

That's so they can play
hide-and-seek in apple trees.

Some monsters choose yellow.

Yellow monsters like to hide in daffodils.

Some monsters choose blue.

Blue monsters like
to hide in the sky.

Some monsters choose green.

Green monsters like to hide in the grass.

Some monsters choose purple.

Purple monsters like to hide in grapevines.

Some monsters choose orange.

Orange monsters like to hide in
pumpkin patches.

And some monsters choose pink.

Pink monsters like to hide in pink pillows.

Hey! Here's a monster who hasn't chosen a color yet.

What color do you think she'll be?
Look! She's trying red.

Now she's trying yellow.

Uh-oh! She's going for blue, too!

And now she's trying green.

Guess what! She's all those colors!
But where can she hide?

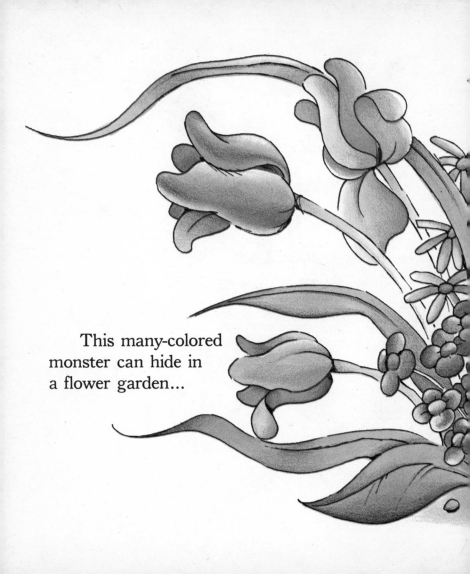

This many-colored
monster can hide in
a flower garden...

...or she can hide in a crowd of monsters!